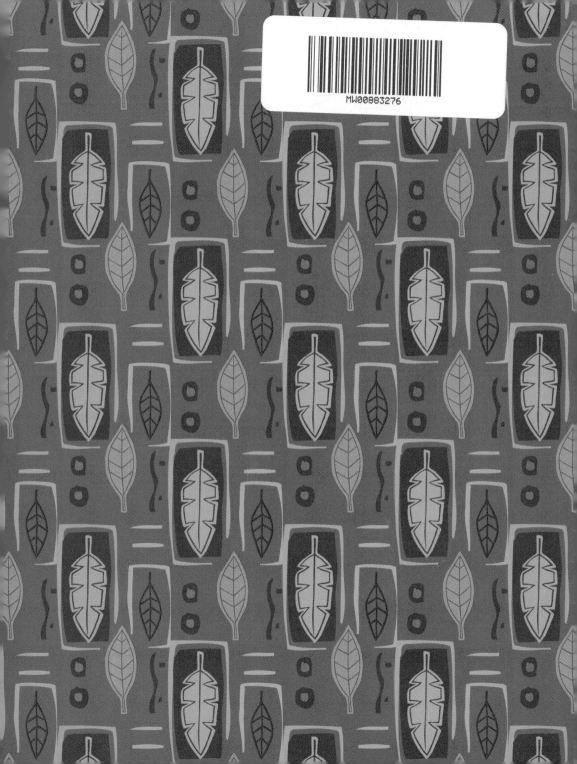

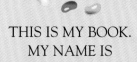

THIS IS MY BOOK.
MY NAME IS

_____

Jungle Rhymes

By Jennifer Liberts • Cover illustrated by Mark Marderosian and Robbin Cuddy

Interior illustrated by Disney Storybook Artists

Random House 🏠 New York

Copyright © 2001 by Disney Enterprises, Inc. All rights reserved under International and Pan-American Copyright Conventions. Tarzan®: Copyright © 2001 Edgar Rice Burroughs, Inc., and Disney Enterprises, Inc. All Rights Reserved. Published in the United States by Random House, Inc., New York, and simultaneously in Canada by Random House of Canada Limited, Toronto, in conjunction with Disney Enterprises, Inc.
TARZAN®
Owned by Edgar Rice Burroughs, Inc., and Used by Permission
Library of Congress Catalog Card Number: 00-107385   ISBN: 0-7364-1128-3
www.randomhouse.com/kids/disney   www.disneybooks.com
Printed in the United States of America   February 2001   10 9 8 7 6 5 4 3 2 1
JELLYBEAN BOOKS, RANDOM HOUSE, and the Random House colophon are registered trademarks and the Jellybean Books colophon is a trademark of Random House, Inc.

Simba Learns a Lesson

Simba was a prince,
Born into royalty.
Rafiki raised him high
For everyone to see.

One day he would be king
And regal, strong, and good.
Still, he had a lot to learn
To rule as lions should.

But Simba wanted to be free
To pounce and run all day.
Mufasa warned, "Stay close to home."
But Simba longed to stray.

So he sneaked to a secret place,
With Nala by his side.

When out jumped some hyenas!
There was no place to hide!

Simba tried to swipe his claws
To chase the beasts away.

But Mufasa's mighty roar
Really saved the day.

Under a sky filled with stars,
Simba learned that night
Putting a friend in danger is wrong,
But telling the truth is right.

Mowgli Makes a Friend

In a quiet jungle place,
Bagheera found a babe asleep.

The wolves all called him Mowgli.
They had a Man-cub to keep.

Mowgli loved his childhood friends.
The animals all loved him, too.

He ate bananas and climbed trees,
And made fast friends with Baloo.

This boy and bear were so alike.
They laughed and talked all day.

They knew they always
would be friends,
Because they both knew
how to play!

Tarzan Fits In

Kala heard a baby's cry
High up in a spreading tree.
She left all of her fellow apes
To see what it might be.

Kala brought the baby home.
She hoped the others wouldn't mind.
She planned to keep the baby,
Although he was a different kind.

Tarzan grew and learned the ropes.
He soon was swinging upside down.
He entertained the apes that way.
Sometimes he acted like a clown.

Tarzan still felt different, though.
He really wasn't an ape.
His body wasn't hairy,
And he was a different shape.

But Kala really loved her boy.
She said, "We share a special part,
For deep inside of all of us,
There is a loving heart!"

Is your child ready to read?
Move on up to Step into Reading® Books!